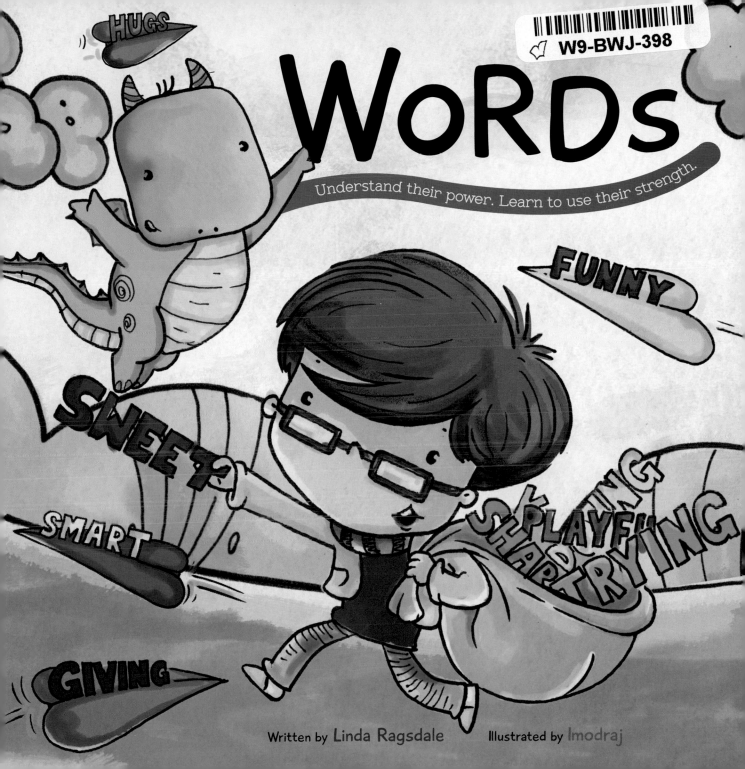

May you fill yourself with kind words and always remember to make your words count.

Designed by Flowerpot Press in Franklin, TN.
www.FlowerpotPress.com
Designer: Stephanie Meyers
Editor: Katrine Crow
ROR-0808-0100
ISBN: 978-1-4867-1254-0
Made in China/Fabriqué en Chine

There is nothing a Peace Dragon likes better than teaching and learning about peace.

Words are a key to peace, and we learn all about them in the pages of this book.

So come on inside...it's peaceful in here.

If an angry word heads your way, move to the side.
Mean words don't work if they miss their mark.

Call yourself SMART for stepping out of the way.

If a hateful word tries to snag your ears, close them, and hum a fun song. Mean words don't get in if you don't pay attention.

Call yourself a **CHAMPION** for singing your own tune.

If a harsh word stings a friend, send a nice word their way.
A nice word can heal the hurt.

Call yourself HERO for making someone feel strong.

If a mean word should happen to sneak its way through
and become a mean spark,
boiling, and spoiling, and spewing its way out of you...

...then take your KIND words and use them to cool and calm the burn.

Call yourself HUMAN because it happens to everyone.

Fill yourself with kind words...
by the handful,
by the head-full,
by the heart-full.

Then give them away...
...in a wish, in a whisper, in a "WAHOO!"

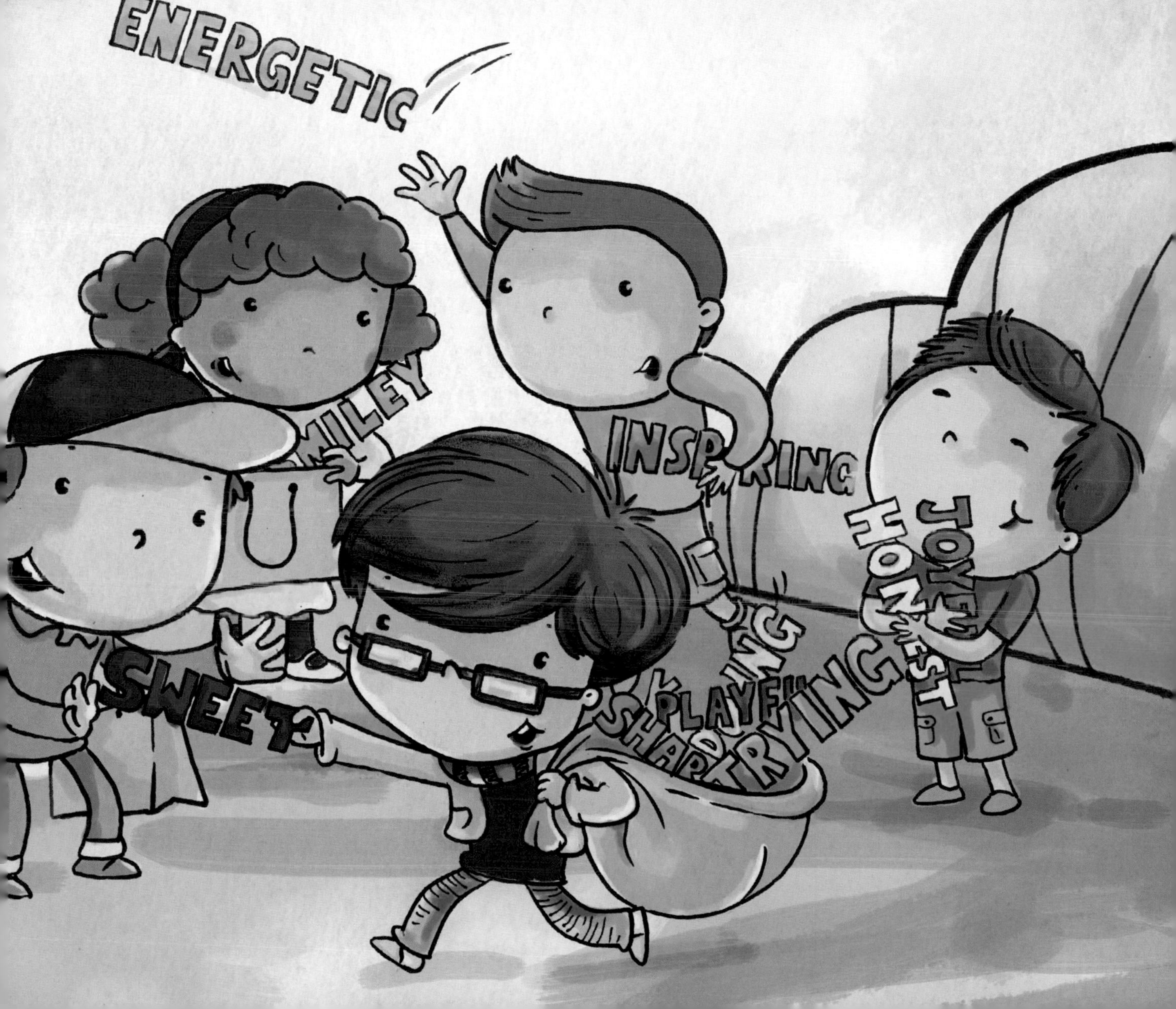

Call yourself FRIEND, because kind words
are gifts that brighten everyone's day.

Words have a power only you can control.

They can heal or hurt, build or burn.

It's not what they say to you that matters—
it's what you say to others,
and what you say to yourself.

FUNNY

It's what you call others,
and what you call yourself.

Make your words count.

Hi! I'm Pax. I'm a Peace Dragon.

My very favorite thing in the entire world is to fly around the world and encourage people to be peacemakers, like in these books. Did you know that everyone can be a peacemaker? If you choose to see, speak, and act through a kind heart and calm thoughts, YOU are a peacemaker! Once you practice, it's easy—and pretty fun, too!

We all have times where we need help choosing peace, such as learning to work with people who are different than we are, or dealing with unkind words that come our way. By reading and thinking about ways to choose kindness or peace before a challenge comes our way, it helps us be prepared to choose peace.

By practicing awesome peaceful solutions, we become examples of love, while building a foundation of peacemaking that will last a lifetime.

HUGS,

Pax